HOSTEL

A HORROR DETECTIVE STORY

KHWAIRAKPAM GOUTAM SINGH

To my friends, colleagues, and all near and dear ones,

This book is dedicated to each of you who finds joy and intrigue in the chilling embrace of horror stories, the enigmatic allure of crime and detective narratives, and the timeless pleasure of reading. Your love for the macabre, the mysterious, and the written word has inspired the creation of this tale, and it is with gratitude and excitement that I share it with you.

With deepest appreciation and warmest regards, Khwairakpam Goutam Singh.

Contents

FOREWORD

The opportunity to share this story with you through such a reputable publishing house is an honour and a joy. Writing fiction allows me to explore new realms of creativity and adds a refreshing dimension to my life.

This journey into the world of fiction has been both exhilarating and enlightening. It has allowed me to weave narratives that entertain, provoke thought, and evoke emotions. Each story is a new adventure, a chance to delve into the human experience uniquely and meaningfully.

I am immensely grateful for the support and encouragement from friends, family, and colleagues throughout this process. Their belief in my work has been a source of great motivation. I also extend my heartfelt thanks to the publishing house for their trust and for giving this story a platform to reach readers far and wide.

As you turn these pages, I hope you will find the same joy and excitement in reading this story as I did in writing it. May it offer you new perspectives, moments of reflection, and a pleasurable escape into the world of imagination.

I look forward to continuing this journey and sharing more stories. Thank you for joining me in this endeavour.

Preface

Within the sinister depths of the forest, a tale of horror and redemption unfolds within the walls of a haunted hostel. As you embark on this chilling journey, prepare to be drawn into a world shrouded in the echoes of unspeakable terror and the enduring pursuit of justice.

In this harrowing lair, Simon, a courageous student, and Johny the Sniffer, a detective with an unwavering dedication to truth, converge in a relentless quest to unravel the mysteries that have festered within the hostel's malevolent embrace. Guided by the restless spirit of a student seeking retribution for a terrible fate, they navigate through a labyrinth of unsettling hints and dark truths, determined to hold the avaricious owner accountable for his heinous deeds.

As the story unfolds, the haunting legacy of the hostel's history of torture and murder comes to a gripping climax, delivering justice for the innocent and solace for the grieving. Through the interplay of darkness and light, sorrow and triumph, this tale invites you to explore the depths of the human spirit and the enduring power of courage in the face of malevolence.

ACKNOWLEDGEMENTS

The story and characters in this book are entirely fictional and not based on any real events, individuals, or institutions. Any resemblance to actual persons, living or dead, or any entity is purely coincidental. The author intends no harm or offense to anyone and is solely responsible for the content of this work.This book is a product of imagination and not meant to be taken as a representation of reality.

Prologue

Deep within the ancient and forbidding woods, a haunted hostel stood as a monument to unspeakable horrors. Its walls bore witness to a history of torment and bloodshed orchestrated by the hostel's avaricious owner, whose insatiable greed drove him to entice and ensnare unsuspecting students.

Among these students was Simon, a young man whose courage and curiosity led him into the clutches of the malevolent hostel. Little did he know that his fate would become entwined with that of Johny the Sniffer, a detective renowned for his unyielding determination to uncover the truth, no matter how dark or elusive.

In the heart of this haunting lair, Johny found himself drawn to the enigmatic riddles surrounding the hostel, sensing that the key to its mysteries lay hidden within its walls. As he delved into the labyrinth of unsettling hints and dark truths, he was assisted and clued by a restless spirit, the ethereal presence of a student whose own tragic fate had bound him to the hostel, seeking justice for the atrocities committed within its confines.

Together, the spirit guided Johny and Simon through the treacherous maze of secrets, leading them toward the heart of the hostel's darkness. Their quest for justice became entwined with the spirit's desire for retribution as they sought to bring the killer to account for the terrible fate that had befallen the innocent.

In the end, the greedy owner met with the consequences of his heinous deeds, and justice was delivered for the deceased student, bringing both tears and smiles to the hearts of his grieving parents. Having fulfilled its purpose, the spirit found solace in the justice served and departed from the mortal realm, leaving behind a lingering sense of closure and redemption in the wake of the hostel's harrowing legacy.

I
Chapter-1
Introduction

The boys' hostel stood like a haunted monument, isolated and forsaken, in the remote outskirts of the university town. Nestled among the whispering woods and rolling hills, it seemed to exist in a world of its own, far removed from the bustling campus life. With its gleaming buildings and vibrant student body, the university lay a mere 3 kilometres away, yet the hostel felt like a different planet. The winding road that connected the two was often shrouded in mist as if trying to keep the hostel's dark secrets hidden from prying eyes.

The hostel's history was marred by tragedy. Several workers had lost their lives during its construction, victims of strange accidents and unexplained occurrences. The locals whispered of curses and malevolent spirits, warning of the hostel's dark energy. Yet, the university had deemed it fit for students, and the boys' hostel had become a place of dread, where fear and anxiety lingered in every corner.

The isolation, the eerie atmosphere, and the tragic history had all combined to make the hostel a place where terror lurked in every shadow, waiting to strike. And now, with the recent suicide of a student, the hostel seemed to be awakening from its slumber, ready to unleash a fresh wave of horror upon its unsuspecting inhabitants.

The wealthy and influential businessman, Mr. Thakuram, owned the university and the hostel. He had built his empire through shady deals and connections with influential politicians and criminals. The construction of the hostel had been rushed, with safety protocols ignored and corner-cutting measures taken to maximise profits. The workers' deaths had been conveniently labelled as accidents, and the families had been silenced with hush money.

II

Chapter-2 The Ghostly Secrets of Thakuram's Hostel: Simon's Awakening

Simon Mathew, a bright-eyed and ambitious freshman, had just received the news he had been dreading - he had been allotted a seat in the notorious boys' hostel. As he stepped out of the university administration building, the misty wind whispered ominous tales in his ear, and the trees leaned in as if listening to his every thought. Simon had heard the rumours, the whispers of ghostly apparitions, unexplained noises, and strange occurrences that plagued the hostel. But he had always been sceptical, dismissing the stories as mere fabrications.

Yet, as he made his way to the hostel, his heart raced with a mix of excitement and trepidation. He had always been fascinated by the supernatural and the unknown, and a part of him wondered if the hostel's dark reputation was more than just a myth. Little did he know, he was about to become a part of the hostel's sinister history, and his life would never be the same again.

Simon had heard whispers about Mr. Thakuram's questionable ethics, but he had never imagined that he would be living in a building with such a dark history. He felt a chill run down his spine as he entered the hostel. Something didn't feel right. The gleaming floors and modern amenities couldn't mask the unease permeating the air.

Little did Simon know he was about to uncover secrets that would endanger his life. The hostel was a hub of illegal activities, and Mr. Thakuram's goons kept a close eye on the students, ensuring that no one dared to speak out. Simon's curiosity and determination would soon make him a target, and he would have to fight to survive in a place where the line between good and evil was blurred.

Simon's eyes wandered around the deserted corridors, taking in the eerie silence. The hostel was only four years old, but its reputation had already plummeted. Only twenty students, admitted recently, scattered across the four floors, and the eerie silence was punctuated only by the creaks and groans of the deserted corridors.

The hostel had lost its name, literally. The sign that once proudly displayed its name now hung crookedly, with letters missing or vandalised. It was as if the hostel was trying to erase its identity, to hide the sinister secrets that lurked within the world.

Desperate to revive the hostel's reputation, Mr. Thakuram launched a classy advertising campaign, touting the hostel's modern amenities and luxurious facilities. He offered enticing discounts and free concessions to lure new students, hoping to fill the empty rooms and restore the hostel's former glory.

But Simon soon realised that Mr. Thakuram's motives were far from altruistic. The owner (Thakuram) had a hidden agenda - to lure enough students to the hostel, wait until the rumours of paranormal activity died down, and then hike up the fees to exploit the students. It was a clever ploy allowing Mr. Thakuram to profit from the students' suffering.

Simon began noticing strange occurrences as he settled into his new life at the hostel. Doors would slam shut on their own, and disembodied voices whispered in the night. It was as if the hostel was fighting back against Mr. Thakuram's attempts to revive it, determined to bury its dark secrets.

Simon knew he had to be careful. Even in his dreams, a young man persistently tried to convey something to him. He was trapped in a sinister game where the owner's greed and the hostel's malevolent energy were pitted against his survival. He had to uncover the truth behind the hostel's cursed reputation before it was too late or risk becoming another victim of its deadly secrets.

Simon felt a chill run down his spine as he realised he was living in a place where fear and anxiety lingered in every corner. The hostel seemed to be awakening, its malevolent energy stirring once more. He discovered that the deceased student from his dreams was recognisable from group photos displayed in an abandoned room of the hostel. And Simon was right in the middle of it all, a mere pawn in a game of horror and survival.

III

Chapter-3 Greed's Grip: Students Caught in a Web of Deception

Unbeknownst to Simon, the other 20 students who had taken up residence in the hostel were also beginning to experience strange and terrifying occurrences. Some reported finding eerie symbols etched into the walls, while others heard disembodied whispers in the dead of night.

As the days passed, the students realised they had all been lured to the hostel under false pretenses. Mr. Thakuram's promises of a comfortable and safe living environment had been nothing more than a ruse, a clever trap designed to ensnare vulnerable students.

The students were now trapped, stuck in a living nightmare from which there seemed no escape. They began to band together, sharing their experiences and trying to make sense of the sinister forces that appeared to be at work in the hostel.

But, as they delved deeper into the mystery, they realised they were in grave danger. Mr. Thakuram's true intentions were far more sinister than they could have imagined, and the hostel's dark energy was growing stronger by the day.

The students knew they had to act fast to uncover the truth behind the hostel's cursed reputation and escape before it was too late. But, as they fought to survive, they realised that the hostel had a mind of its own, and it would stop at nothing to claim their souls. They were helpless.

Simon and the other students had left their rural villages and small towns to pursue their dreams of higher education. Their parents had sacrificed everything to support them, sending them with limited money and prayer.

But, they found themselves trapped in a nightmarish situation, with no escape from the hostel's clutches. They were far from home, with no financial safety net and no support system to turn to. Mr. Thakuram knew this, and he exploited their vulnerability ruthlessly.

The students' desperation and fear were palpable, and the hostel seemed to feed on their negative emotions. As they struggled to survive, they realised that they were not just fighting against the hostel's dark energy but also against the cruel fate that had brought them to this place.

With no one to turn to, they banded together, sharing what little resources they had and trying to find a way out of the hostel's deadly grasp. But, as they fought for survival, they knew their chances of escape were slim, and the hostel's dark secrets seemed to be closing in on them.

Simon and his fellow students were academic stars, shining bright with their intellect and potential. But, unbeknownst to them, they were pawns in a sinister game. The owner of the university and hostel had a cunning plan to exploit their talent for his gain.

Thakuram lured them in with promises of a quality education and comfortable living, but his true intention was to use their academic success to boost the hostel and university's reputation. He would then hike the fees, making it impossible for poor students to afford, and create a lucrative business model catering only to the wealthy.

The owner planned to showcase the students' achievements to attract more students and then trap them in his web of greed. He would advertise the university and hostel as a hub of excellence, but in reality, it was a den of exploitation.

Simon and his friends were caught in this trap, their brilliance and hard work being used to further the owner's selfish ambitions. They were unaware of the evil plan but soon faced a harsh reality that would shake their trust in the system forever.

The truth began to unravel when Simon stumbled upon a cryptic message scrawled on a hidden wall in the hostel, written in blood: 'I didn't jump, I was pushed.' The message was eerie and chilling, and Simon knew it was a desperate cry for help from a former student.

As Simon dug deeper, he discovered a shocking truth. The student who had supposedly committed suicide earlier had been subjected to brutal torture by Mr. Thakuram himself, driven to the brink of madness and ultimately killed by the unbearable pain. The suicide note was a fabrication, a cover-up to conceal the heinous crime.

Simon's heart raced as he realised the true extent of Mr. Thakuram's cruelty. He had lured brilliant students to his institution only to exploit and torture them for his twisted gratification. The hostel, once a symbol of hope and learning, had become a chamber of horrors due to the greediness and lush for the money.

With this knowledge, Simon knew he had to act quickly. He couldn't let Mr. Thakuram keep exploiting innocent students. As he planned his next move, he felt the heavy, dark presence of the hostel's owner pressing down on him. He was in danger, and he knew it. But Simon was a fearless young man.

The truth about the suicide student's past began to unravel, revealing a heartbreaking tale of exploitation and cruelty. Like Simon, he had been lured to the hostel with promises of free education and accommodation. But, after a year of excelling in his studies, Mr. Thakuram had turned on him, demanding payment for the 'favours' he had received. Coming from a destitute family, the student had no means to pay. He was trapped, and Mr. Thakuram took advantage of his vulnerability, subjecting him to daily torture and even sexual assault.

IV
Chapter-4 Seeking Redemption

Ramu, Simon's distant relative, a contractual sweeper at the police station, had arrived at the hostel, concerned about Simon's well-being. As they embraced, Simon shared his terrifying experiences at the hostel. Ramu's eyes widened in shock, and he quickly pulled out his phone. 'I need to call someone,' he said. 'Someone who can help us uncover the truth.'

He dialled a number, and a gruff voice answered. 'Johny, my friend, I need your expertise. Simon, my relative, is in trouble. He's being exploited and tortured at this hostel.' Ramu listened for a moment before handing the phone to Simon. 'Tell Johny everything,' he urged.

Simon hesitated but began to recount his story to the mysterious Johny, also known as 'Sniffer', due to his incredible detective skills. As he spoke, he felt a glimmer of hope. Maybe, just maybe, he could escape this nightmare with Johny's help.

Johny, known as 'Sniffer', was Ramu's best friend and a renowned detective. He had a reputation for solving the most challenging cases with his exceptional skills and keen instincts. As Simon shared his story, Johny listened intently, his mind already racing with theories and suspects.

'Don't worry, Simon,' Johny said, his voice firm and reassuring. 'We'll get to the bottom of this. Ramu, let's visit Mr Thakuram and see what he says for himself.'

Ramu nodded, and together, they devised a plan to confront Mr. Thakuram and expose the truth. Simon felt a surge of gratitude towards Ramu and Johny, knowing he wasn't alone in this fight anymore. With their help, he was determined to bring Mr. Thakuram to justice and free himself and the other students from the hostel's clutches.

Johny's eyes narrowed as he watched Mr. Thakuram's every move. The detective's instincts were screaming that something was amiss. He noticed the way Mr. Thakuram avoided eye contact, his hands trembled somewhat as he gestured, and the overly sweet tone in his voice.

'I see,' Johny said, his voice dripping with scepticism. 'Well, in that case, I'm sure you won't mind if we look around. Ramu, let's split up and cover more ground.'

Ramu nodded, and the two began to search the hostel, looking for evidence that might support Simon's claims. Johny's eyes scanned every nook and cranny, taking in the worn furniture, the peeling paint, and the eerie silence that seemed to permeate the very walls.

As they searched, Johny's suspicions only grew stronger. He knew they were getting close to uncovering the truth, and he was determined to expose Mr. Thakuram's secrets once and for all.

Johny's eyes widened as he took in the gruesome message. 'I didn't jump. I was pushed,' he read aloud, his voice barely above a whisper. Ramu's face was pale, his eyes fixed on the bloodstained words.

'This changes everything,' Johny said, his mind racing with the implications. 'The student's death wasn't a suicide. It was murder.'

Ramu nodded, his eyes scanning the room as if searching for more clues. 'We need to find out who wrote this,' he said, his voice firm. 'And who they're trying to protect.'

Johny's eyes locked onto the message again, his mind working overtime. The case was no longer just a case of exploitation. It was a murder investigation. And he was determined to get to the bottom of it.

Johny's phone rang as he waited for the forensic team to arrive. He answered, listening intently as the coroner's office confirmed his suspicions. 'The post-mortem report shows signs of struggle and blunt force trauma, inconsistent with a suicide,' the coroner said.

Johny's eyes met Ramu's, and he knew they were on the same page. The case was a homicide, and they had a killer to catch.

The forensic team arrived, and Johny led them to the scene. They collected samples of the bloodstained message, and Johny requested a rush on the DNA analysis.

As they waited for the results, Johny's mind raced with theories. Who was the killer? And what was their motive? He knew the answers lay in the evidence and was determined to uncover them.

The DNA report confirmed Johny's suspicions. The bloodstains on the wall matched the DNA of the victim.

Johny's eyes narrowed as he pieced together the evidence. 'We have a breakthrough,' he said to Ramu, his voice firm. 'This changes everything.'

Ramu's eyes widened in anticipation. 'What does it mean?'

Johny's face was grim. 'It means we're dealing with something much bigger than we thought. Let's get back to the station and analyse the evidence further. We need to uncover the truth behind this tragic event,' he told Ramu.

The DNA report confirmed Johny's suspicions. The bloodstains on the wall matched the DNA of the victim, and the writing on the wall seemed to scream for justice.

Johny's eyes widened as he realised the truth. 'This isn't just a message,' he said to Ramu, his voice barely above a whisper. 'It's a cry for help from beyond the grave.'

Ramu's face paled as he understood. 'You mean...the student's spirit is trying to communicate with us?'

Johnny nodded, his eyes locked on the writing. 'The torture, the suffering... it's all connected. The student's soul is trying to guide us to the truth, to ensure justice is served.' He had encountered many such cases before, though they often fell outside legal boundaries.

The air in the room seemed to grow colder as if the student's spirit was watching them and waiting for them to uncover the truth.

Meanwhile, Mr. Thakuram was getting increasingly anxious. He knew the writing on the wall was a dead giveaway, and he had to act fast to cover his tracks. He tried to devise a plan to divert the investigation and shift the focus away from himself.

He paced back and forth in his office, his mind racing with ideas. He could claim that the student was mentally unstable and that he had a history of hallucinations and paranoia. Or he could try to bribe the investigators and offer them a hefty sum to look the other way.

But deep down, he knew it was only a matter of time before the truth came out. He had gone too far and was now trapped in his own web of deceit. The student's spirit was not going to let him escape that easily.

Mr. Thakuram's attempts to divert the investigation were futile. The student's spirit relentlessly pursued justice, and Johny was hot on the trail. With his keen detective skills and unwavering determination, Johny was closing in on the truth.

The higher authorities were watching with bated breath, aware that Johny was a force to be reckoned with. They had seen him take down corrupt officials before and knew he wouldn't hesitate to do it again if necessary.

Johny's reputation as a fearless and incorruptible detective had earned him both respect and fear from those in power. They knew that if he uncovered any wrongdoing, he would not hesitate to expose it, no matter how high up the chain it went.

The student's spirit and Johny were a formidable force against the killer, and Mr. Thakuram ran out of options. The noose tightened around him, and he knew his time was running out.

As the investigation closed in, the student's spirit grew more restless. It began to exact a terrifying revenge on Mr. Thakuram, haunting his every waking moment.

Disembodied whispers echoed in his mind, 'You will pay for what you did.' Shadows moved in the corners of his eyes, and he felt an icy presence lurking just out of sight.

Mr. Thakuram tried to flee, but the spirit was relentless. It conjured visions of the student's tortured face, his eyes screaming in agony. The sound of his own screams echoed in Mr. Thakuram's mind, driving him to the brink of madness.

Johny watched as Mr. Thakuram's composure crumbled, his eyes sunken with fear. He knew the spirit was demanding its own brand of justice, and he was powerless to stop it.

The killer's torment was a grim reminder that some crimes went far beyond human punishment and that the spirits of the dead would not rest until justice was served.

Johny's next lead took him to the student's grief-stricken parents. He found them in a state of utter devastation, their world shattered by the loss of their child.

With compassion and sensitivity, Johny interviewed them, piecing together the student's final days. The parents revealed their son's fears and anxieties, his struggles with the hostel's harsh environment, and his cries for help that went unheeded.

Johny's eyes narrowed as he listened, his mind racing with theories. He pressed for more information, asking about anyone who might have had a grudge against their son.

The father hesitated, then revealed a shocking detail: 'Our son had discovered something sinister in the hostel, something he wouldn't tell us about. He was too afraid.'

Johny's grip on his pen tightened. 'What was it?' he asked, his voice firm but gentle.

The mother's eyes welled up with tears. 'We don't know, but our son's spirit won't rest until we find out.'

Johny's heart went out to the family, struggling to make ends meet and powerless to protect their son. They had been trapped in a cycle of poverty and fear, unable to escape the hostel's clutches.

The mother's eyes pleaded with Johny, 'We knew something was wrong, but we couldn't afford to take him out of the hostel. We were trapped, just like our son.'

Johny's determination grew. He vowed to expose the hostel's dark secrets, to bring justice to the family and closure to the student's spirit.

The mother's voice cracked, 'He said...he said they were torturing him for the fees, that he was begging us to take him out of the hostel and the university. But we couldn't, we just couldn't. We didn't have the means.'

Johny's eyes narrowed, his mind racing with the implications. Torture for fees? The hostel's sinister secrets unravelled, and Johny was determined to expose them all.

Meanwhile, the student's spirit was relentless in its pursuit of justice. It haunted Mr. Thakuram's every waking moment, its presence a constant reminder of his heinous crime.

The spirit's wrath was unforgiving, tormenting Mr. Thakuram day and night. It invaded his dreams, conjuring visions of the student's tortured face, his eyes screaming in agony.

V
Chapter-5
Confession in the Dark

Mr. Thakuram's sanity began to unravel, his mind shattered by the spirit's unyielding vengeance. He became a shadow of his former self, haunted by the ghost of his own guilt.

The spirit's presence was a constant whisper in his ear, 'You will never escape, you will never be free.' And in that darkness, Mr. Thakuram knew he was doomed to suffer, trapped in a living hell of his own making.

Desperate to escape the spirit's wrath, Mr. Thakuram sought the help of powerful evil tantrics (Evil tantrics, often referred to as dark or black magicians, are practitioners of certain esoteric rituals and occult practices in the realm of tantra who use their knowledge and powers for malevolent purposes. Unlike genuine tantra, which is a spiritual practice aimed at enlightenment and self-realisation, evil tantrics pervert these practices to harm others, control spirits, manipulate energy for selfish gain, or inflict suffering), paying vast sums of money to rid himself of the student's ghostly presence.

But the spirit was not to be underestimated. It fought back with ferocity, engaging the evil tantrics in a spectacular battle of supernatural forces.

The air was filled with the sound of clashing energies as the spirit's fury clashed with the tantrics' dark magic. The hostel walls shook, and the ground trembled as the two forces battled for dominance.

Despite their best efforts, the tantrics were no match for the spirit's righteous anger. They fled in terror one by one, their dark arts no match for the student's unyielding determination.

And so, the spirit remained, its presence a constant reminder to Mr. Thakuram of his crime, and the consequences that awaited him.

Mr. Thakuram, desperate and depraved, sought out the darkest of arts, calling upon foreign evil tantrics who wielded malevolent powers. He paid a fortune to enlist their aid, sacrificing his last shreds of decency.

The foreign tantrics unleashed a maelstrom of dark energy, striking the student's spirit with unprecedented force. The spirit stumbled, its light flickering in the face of such malevolence.

But just as all seemed lost, a chorus of whispers echoed through the hostel, a gathering of restless spirits, victims of similar injustices, who had been watching and waiting.

United in their quest for justice, the spirits of the aggrieved joined forces, their collective energy bolstering the student's spirit. Together, they counterattacked, a blazing storm of righteous fury that repelled the evil tantrics and shattered Mr. Thakuram's last defences.

With the dark tantrics vanquished, the student's spirit turned to its newfound allies, its ethereal form wavering with gratitude. It reached out with spectral hands, gesturing in heartfelt thanks.

The other spirits, understanding the depth of the student's appreciation, responded in kind. They waved back, their own ghostly hands fluttering in a poignant display of solidarity.

The student's spirit nodded, its presence shimmering with emotion. It mouthed a silent 'thank you', its voice barely audible over the whispering wind.

As the other spirits began to fade away, the student's spirit watched, its gaze filled with a deep sense of connection. It knew it was no longer alone and that others understood its pain and its quest for justice.

With renewed strength and determination, the student's spirit unleashed a fierce wrath upon Mr. Thakuram. The killer's screams echoed through the hostel as the spirit's vengeance intensified.

The spirit's anger was palpable, its presence crackling with electricity. It conjured visions of the student's final moments, forcing Mr. Thakuram to relive the horror he had unleashed.

The killer's mind reeled, his sanity fraying under the spirit's relentless assault. He begged for mercy, but the spirit was unforgiving, its wrath a testament to its suffering.

And so, the torture continued, a never-ending cycle of pain and fear, as the student's spirit exacted its revenge upon the man who had wronged it so grievously.

The student's parents arrived at the hostel, drawn by the whispers of strange occurrences and unexplained events. They had heard rumours of a malevolent presence and sought answers from the hostel's owner, Mr. Thakuram.

As they entered the room, they were met with a sight that made their blood run cold. Mr. Thakuram, the man they had trusted with their son's care, was cowering in fear, his eyes haunted by the spirit's wrath.

The mother's cry was piercing, 'What have you done?! What have you done to our son?!' She rushed towards Mr. Thakuram, her hands clawing at him like a wild animal.

The father's face was contorted in rage, 'You monster! You tortured our son! You killed him!' He lunged at Mr. Thakuram, his fists flying in a blur of anger.

The spirit, sensing its parents' presence, paused in its torture. It watched as they vented their grief and anger upon the killer. And in that moment, the spirit knew it had finally found justice.

Mr. Thakuram, the once-confident killer, was now reduced to a snivelling, grovelling mess. He begged for mercy, his eyes streaming with tears, his voice cracking with desperation.

'Please...please forgive me! I didn't mean to hurt your son! I was desperate, I was weak...please, have mercy on me!'

The parents' anger and grief were unrelenting, their faces twisted in disgust and sorrow. They could not bear to look at the man who had tortured and killed their son, who had shattered their lives forever.

'You showed no mercy to our son!' the father roared, his voice echoing off the walls. 'You showed no compassion, no humanity! Why should we show you any mercy now?'

The mother's voice was a cold, calculated whisper. 'You will get no mercy from us. You will get no peace. Our son's spirit will haunt you forever, and so will our wrath.'

As Mr. Thakuram begged for his life, his words struck a chord in the parents' hearts. They had never considered that their son's killer was also a father, that he had children who needed him.

The mother's expression faltered, her eyes wavering with a glimmer of compassion. The father's anger seemed to dissipate, replaced by a hint of sorrow.

'You're a father?' the mother asked, her voice barely above a whisper.

Mr. Thakuram nodded, his eyes welling up with tears. 'Yes, I have two children...they need me...please, don't take me away from them...'

The parents exchanged a glance, their hearts softening despite themselves. They remembered their son, their loss, and the pain that still lingered.

The father's voice was heavy with emotion. 'We will spare your life...but you must face the consequences of your actions. You must live with the guilt of what you've done.'

The mother added, her voice firm but gentle. 'And you must use your life to make amends...to honour our son's memory...to be a better father to your own children.'

The parents' eyes bore into Mr. Thakuram's soul, their gaze unwavering. 'But there is one more thing you must do,' the father said, his voice firm. 'You must confess to the police and surrender to justice. You must face the consequences of your crime and accept the punishment you deserve.'

The mother's voice was resolute. 'You must take responsibility for your actions and honor our son's memory by telling the truth. No more lies, no more deception. The truth, and only the truth.'

Mr. Sharma nodded, his eyes downcast, his shoulders slumped in defeat. 'I will...I will confess...I will surrender...I promise.'

The parents' faces were stern, but their eyes held a glimmer of hope. Hope that justice would be served, their son's memory would be honored, and that Mr. Thakuram would find redemption, no matter how small, for his heinous crime.

With a sense of resignation and defeat, Mr. Thakuram rushed into the police station, his hands shaking and his eyes cast down. He approached the front desk, where a stern-looking officer greeted him.

'I want to surrender,' Mr. Thakuram said, his voice barely audible. 'I want to confess to a crime.'

The officer raised an eyebrow. 'What crime?'

Mr. Thakuram took a deep breath. 'The murder of a student...at the hostel...I was the one...'

Just then, a tall, imposing figure emerged from the shadows. It was Johny, the detective, his eyes piercing and his jaw set in a firm line.

'Ah, Mr. Thakuram,' Johny said, his voice firm. 'I've been expecting you. You see, I've been investigating a certain...mysterious occurrence...at the hostel. And your name kept coming up.'

Mr. Thakuram's eyes widened in fear as Johny's gaze bore into him. He knew he was trapped and that the detective would uncover the truth.

Mr. Thakuram's eyes dropped, his shoulders slumping in defeat. 'Yes, I did it,' he whispered to Johny. 'I killed the student. I was desperate, I was angry...I greedy.'

VI

Chapter-6 The Ghostly Judgment: Thakuram's Last Stand

The courtroom was packed as Mr. Thakuram stood before the judge, his head bowed in shame. The prosecutor read out the charges, and Mr. Thakuram's voice was barely audible as he replied, 'Guilty'.

The judge's face was stern, her eyes piercing. 'You have confessed to the heinous crime of murdering a young student. You have shown no remorse and no empathy for the victim's family. You have only shown cowardice and a lack of humanity.'

Mr. Thakuram's eyes dropped, his shoulders slumped in defeat. 'I know, your honor. I am ashamed of what I have done. I am willing to accept the consequences of my actions.'

The judge's voice was firm. 'Very well. I hereby sentence you to life imprisonment without the possibility of parole. You will spend the rest of your days in prison, reflecting on the gravity of your crime.'

As the judge's words echoed through the courtroom, the parents of the deceased student felt a sense of closure, a sense of justice finally served. They had waited for this moment for so long, and now that it had finally arrived, they felt a mix of emotions.

VII
Chapter-7
Conclusion

Parents tears streamed down their faces as they smiled, a smile of relief, of gratitude, of closure. They held each other tight, their arms wrapped around each other, as they whispered words of comfort and support.

Their son's memory would never be forgotten, but now they could finally start to heal, to move on from the tragedy that had befallen them. They knew that their son's spirit was at peace and that justice had been served.

The mother's voice was barely audible as she whispered, 'Our son can finally rest in peace.' The father nodded, his eyes red from crying, as he replied, 'Yes, our son is finally at peace.'

As the parents smiled through their tears, a faint light emanated from the back of the courtroom. The spirit of their son, who had been present throughout the trial, began to take shape.

His eyes shone with a bright light, a warm smile spreading across his face. He looked at his parents, and they felt a sense of peace over them.

The spirit began to glow brighter, his form becoming more defined. He raised a hand, and his parents felt a gentle touch on their faces.

And then, in an instant, he was gone. The light enveloped him, and he vanished into its brilliance. The courtroom was silent, the only sound the soft sobbing of the parents.

But they were not tears of sadness. They were tears of joy and relief, knowing their son was finally at peace. They knew he was no longer trapped between worlds and was finally free to move on.

The parents smiled at each other, their hearts full of gratitude. They knew they would always carry their son's memory with them, but they also knew he was finally home.

And so, the wheels of justice had turned, and the truth had finally been revealed. But as the dust settled, new questions began to emerge, and the journey for answers was far from over. The story of the tragic events at the hostel would continue, with secrets yet to be uncovered and a legacy of truth yet to be revealed.

www.ingramcontent.com/pod-product-compliance
Lightning Source LLC
Chambersburg PA
CBHW021150130726
47988CB00004B/1547